a minedition book
published by Penguin Young Readers Group

Text and illustrations copyright © 2007 by Chisato Tashiro
English text translation by Sayako Uchida and Kate Westerlund
Coproduction with Michael Neugebauer Publishing Ltd., Hong Kong.
Rights arranged with "minedition" Rights and Licensing AG, Zurich, Switzerland.
Published simultaneously in Canada.
Manufactured in China by Wide World Ltd.
Typesetting in Baskerville.
Color separation by Fotoreproduzioni Grafiche, Verona, Italy.
Library of Congress Cataloging-in-Publication Data available upon request.
Special Market ISBN 978-0-698-40083-2 Not for resale
For more information please visit our website: www.minedition.com

This Imagination Library edition is published by Penguin Group (USA), a Pearson
company, exclusively for Dolly Parton's Imagination Library, a not-for-profit
program designed to inspire a love of reading and learning, sponsored in part by The
Dollywood Foundation. Penguin's trade editions of this work are available wherever
books are sold.

CHISATO

Translated from
the Japanese by
Sayako Uchida

Adapted by
Kate Westerlund

5
NICE
MICE

One night when the moon was full
five little mice heard the sound of music carried by the wind.
"Where is it coming from?" they wanted to know.
Well, there was only one way to find out.
So they began to follow the sound.
They walked through the city, listening in all directions.

They followed the sound to the gates of the park.

The street was dark, but the music was getting louder and louder.

"This must be it," said one.

"Here is a sign," said another.

"What's it say?" asked the youngest.

FROG CONCERT
FROGS ONLY!
"Oh, no!" said the youngest.
"We'll just have to sneak in," said
the oldest.

And that's exactly what they did.
Peeking through the grass they saw a wonderful sight—
a chorus of frogs, all singing a song to the moon.

Gleaming beams of silver carry our tune
farther and farther, up over the moon

The melody was lovely.

Then a voice behind them boomed,
"Can't you read the sign? Frogs only! Out you go!"
So they left.

That night the five little mice couldn't sleep.
The concert had been so exciting and the music
so lovely.
"Wouldn't it be great if we could do that too,"
said the little gray mouse.
They all tried to sing the *Over the Moon* song.
But all that came out was peeping and squeaking.
It didn't sound like the beautiful frog music at all.
"We could play the music on our own instruments,"
said the brown mouse who always had her best
ideas at night.
"Brilliant!" said the oldest. "But what instruments?"

The next morning they all set out to find the things
they needed to make their instruments.

They looked for things
that would cling and clang,

...rustle and rattle

and even things that could tap, tap, boom.

The five little mice worked a long
time building their instruments,
and when they were finished,
they began to practice.
They practiced song after song
until each one was just right.

At last they were ready.
The five little mice put up posters all over the city
to invite everyone to their first concert.
When the big night arrived,
they packed up their instruments and
drove to the concert hall.

They nervously set up their instruments
on stage. Would anybody come to their
concert?
They had to hurry, soon the curtain
would open. Then they heard…

**"Ladies and Gentlemen,
The Five Nice Mice!"**

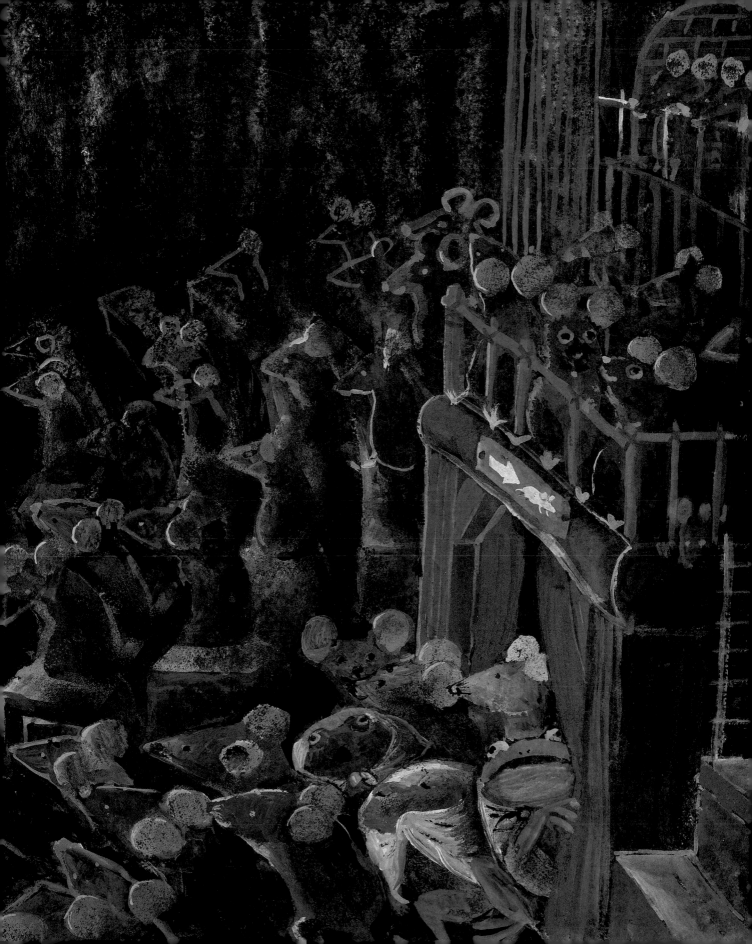

Finally the curtain opened and they began to play,
song after song.

Each one was better than the last.
The audience loved it.

When the concert was over everyone started clapping.
The mice saw their mouse neighbors and relatives, but they
saw some other faces as well.
It was the frogs, and they were trying to hide!
"You don't need to hide," shouted the youngest mouse.
"Come out!"
This caused some confusion, but then the five nice mice said,
"Mouse and frog friends, thank you so much for coming.
We would like to play one more song—
our favorite...*Over the Moon!*"
"You really are five nice mice," said one frog.

They played beautifully.
At first everyone just listened, but then a few of the frogs joined in.
Soon the whole audience began to sing.

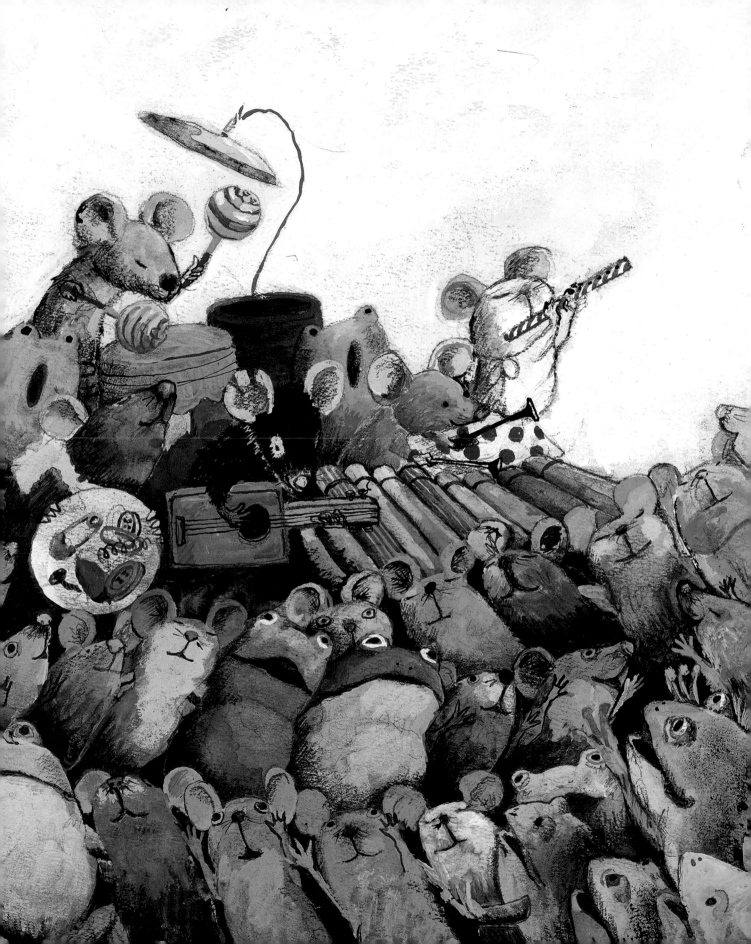

The mice and the frogs created such harmony!
It was a night no one would forget.
And as the morning light began to change the night sky
they all promised to make music together again soon.

And that's what happened.
The next time the moon was full
they played and sang together.

The wind carried their
music farther and farther…
over the moon. They sang
and played together
until they were so tired…
they fell asleep,
mice and frogs together.